The Turn of the Screw

HENRY JAMES

Level 3

Retold by Cherry Gilchrist
Series Editors: Andy Hopkins and Jocelyn Potter

Pearson Education Limited
Edinburgh Gate, Harlow,
Essex CM20 2JE, England
and Associated Companies throughout the world.

ISBN: 978-1-4058-8205-7

This adaptation first published by Penguin Books Ltd 1996
Published by Addison Wesley Longman Ltd and Penguin Books Ltd 1998
New edition first published 1999
This edition first published 2008

Thirteenth Impression 2021

Typeset by Graphicraft Ltd, Hong Kong
Set in 11/14pt Bembo
Printed in Great Britain by Ashford Colour Press Ltd.
SWTC/04

Published by Pearson Education Ltd

Every effort has been made to trace the copyright holders and we apologise in advance
for any unintentional omissions. We would be pleased to insert the appropriate
acknowledgement in any subsequent edition of this publication.

For a complete list of the titles available in the Pearson English Readers series, please
visit www.pearsonenglishreaders.com. Alternatively, write to your local Pearson Education
office or to Pearson English Readers Marketing Department, Pearson Education,
Edinburgh Gate, Harlow, Essex CM20 2JE, England.

Contents

Introduction

'They were a wicked pair,' Mrs Grose said, 'but what can they do now? They're dead.'

'They're still here . . . They can still take Miles and Flora from us!'

A young woman comes to a big country house to teach two young children. It is her first job as a governess and she is alone with the housekeeper, Mrs Grose. Strange things begin to happen. She sees a man on the roof of the house, and a woman by the lake, dressed in black. Mrs Grose can't see them, so the governess describes them to her. They sound like two people who died almost a year ago, Peter Quint and Miss Jessel. These people in black can only be their ghosts. Mrs Grose says that Peter Quint and Miss Jessel were bad people. She says they spent too much time with little Miles and Flora. The two women are very frightened. Have the ghosts come to take the children away? Everyone knows ghosts can't hurt innocent children. But are these beautiful children really innocent?

Henry James wrote this famous story in 1898. He wrote it for an American magazine named *Collier's*. Later he put it into a book. It is one of the most famous ghost stories in English. Benjamin Britten used the story to make a musical play with the same title.

Henry James was an American. He was born in New York in 1843. His father was a well-known writer and speaker, and his brother, William James, was a famous university teacher. As a young man, Henry James studied law at Harvard University. He also travelled widely in Europe. He began to write short stories in 1865. He moved to England in 1876 and stayed there for the rest of his life. He lived in the small town of Rye on the south coast. Many famous writers came to visit him there: Joseph Conrad, Ford Madox Ford and H. G. Wells. Wells became one of his greatest friends. Henry James wrote many famous books: *Washington Square* (1880), *The Portrait of a Lady* (1881), *The Bostonians* (1886), *What Maisie Knew* (1887), *The Wings of the Dove* (1902), *The Ambassadors* (1903) and *The Golden Bowl* (1904). A number of these books have now become films. In 1915, James decided to become British. And in that year, the King of England gave him the *Order of Merit*. This is a special title from the king or queen of England. A few people receive it every year for doing excellent work. James received it because he was an excellent and very successful writer. The following year, James died.

Henry James' books are about people. Some of these people are unhappy or afraid; some of them are in love; some of them want to be rich or famous. The people in his books usually have plenty of money and they like to travel. One of his favourite subjects is young Americans in Europe. In Henry James's time, a lot of young Americans visited Europe and made friends with Europeans. James met a lot of them and was able to watch them and write about them. The Americans in his books are usually rich and hopeful. The Europeans are often clever and selfish; they want to get their hands on the Americans' money. Not many of James's stories have happy endings. By the end, the hopeful people have usually become wiser. They have stopped believing everything that they hear. Most of James's stories take place in the real world. *The Turn of the Screw* is unusual because it is about ghosts.

The title of the book is strange. The word 'screw' has a number of meanings. The most common meaning is a long thin piece of metal that holds pieces of wood or metal together. To push the screw into the wood, you have to turn it round and round with a 'screwdriver'. A long time ago, screws were also used to tighten metal rings on people in prison. When someone turned the screw on the metal ring, the prisoner felt great pain. These screws were used while somebody asked a prisoner questions to get the prisoner's secrets. Even today, prisoners call prison guards 'screws'.

So why did Henry James give the story this title? Here's one possible reason for the title. Perhaps Henry James meant that the story 'turns the screw' on the reader's mind. In other words, the story asks the reader a lot of questions. Are the children really innocent? Or have Quint and Miss Jessel taught them to be bad? And if they really *are* bad, what bad things have they done? Are there really two ghosts who want to take them away? Will the children die? Is the governess doing a good job? Is she looking after them correctly? Or is she useless and unhelpful? We have strong feelings of fear and danger as we read. We aren't sure who is good or bad. And we don't know what is right or wrong.

Here's another possible reason for the title. The governess tells the story. She is sure that the children have secrets. She believes that their secrets are seriously bad. She says they must stop having secrets. She says they should tell her everything. Does she hurt them to learn their secrets? Does she 'turn the screw' on the children that she is looking after?

Even when we get to the end of the story, we are still not able to answer most of these questions. And because of this, the story seems very modern. All these unknown facts form a mystery which we want to think about for a long time. *The Turn of the Screw* is a story that nobody forgets.

Chapter 1   A Governess Gets a Job

It was a strange story which we heard in that old house, on the night before Christmas. We sat by the fire and listened silently until the end. Then somebody said, 'How unusual! It's the first time that I've ever heard about a child who saw a ghost.'

I could see that Douglas wanted to say something. After a few seconds, he spoke. 'It's not the only time that a child has seen a ghost. A ghost story with one child in it is frightening enough. But two children who see ghosts – isn't that quite strange? Doesn't that give the story another turn of the screw?'

'Of course!' somebody answered. 'Two children give two turns of the screw! We want to hear the story!'

Douglas looked at all of us, and said quietly, 'It's a terrible story. It is the most frightening story that I know.'

'Then begin at once!' I said.

'I can't. It's in a book which is locked in my desk at home. I can ask my servant to put it in the post.'

'Oh yes! Please do!' Everyone asked him to hurry.

'Is it your story?' I asked him.

'No, no! I heard it from a woman. I've never forgotten it. She wrote it down, and when she died it came to me. She was ten years older than me. She was my sister's governess when I was a student at university. In the summer holidays I talked to her a lot. Yes – don't smile – she was beautiful. She was also clever and interesting, and I liked her very much. I think she liked me too. It was forty years ago, but I remember everything.'

'Did she tell any others her story?'

'No, she said that I was the first person to hear it.'

The packet arrived in the post two days later. We all wanted to hear the story, and we sat down ready after dinner that evening.

Before Douglas read the story to us, he told us about the young woman. She was twenty years old; she came from a poor, church family, and she decided to work as a governess. She heard about a man who wanted to employ a governess for two children. She went to London and met him at his large house in Harley Street. They were his brother's children; his brother was dead, and now he had to look after them.

The man was handsome, rich, and unmarried, and the young woman was immediately in love with him.

'I'll be so pleased if you can take the job!' he told her. 'London isn't a good place for children. I've taken them to my family home in Essex* – it's a large house with big gardens and a park. I have no time to look after them. I've sent my best servants there, and the housekeeper, Mrs Grose, is a very good woman. You will like her, I'm sure.'

He was very worried about the children, a little girl and her older brother. Not long ago, their first governess died suddenly, and now their uncle had to employ a new governess quickly. He had to find the right person. The boy was away at school, but he came back in the holidays, and the little girl was home all the time.

'How did the first governess die?' a listener asked Douglas. 'Was the job dangerous?'

'You will hear everything,' he answered.

The young lady did not give her answer at once. It was her first job; and the house was big, and almost empty. The money was good, but could she be happy there, alone? She wanted to help this wonderful man, but could she look after the children well enough?

She returned to the house in Harley Street two days later.

'I have decided to take the job,' she said.

* Essex: a part of England in the east of the country.

2

'I'll be so pleased if you can take the job!' he told her.

'Her love for her new master –' somebody said.

'Yes, of course. This love helped her later – it helped her to be brave,' Douglas continued. 'But her employer said, "There's one thing that you must promise me. You must never bring any problem to me. You must never write to me. You must decide everything." '

She promised. He took her hand; he was so pleased with her. She never saw him again.

Douglas opened the red book on his knee, and began to read the governess's story to us.

Chapter 2   The Two Children

I was very worried during the journey. Was I making a mistake? I was going alone to a strange house, to teach two children that I did not know. But it was a beautiful day, and when I arrived, the house was a pleasant surprise. It was large, but light, with open windows and bright flowers in the gardens. And Flora was the most beautiful child that I have ever seen. Her hair was gold in colour, and her dress was blue. She and Mrs Grose, the housekeeper, were there to meet me.

Mrs Grose seemed to be a kind, good woman, and at supper that evening, I asked her about Miles, the boy.

'If you like this little girl, you will like the boy, too,' she said. She smiled at Flora, and Flora smiled at us both. 'He's so clever.'

'When will I see him? Tomorrow?'

'No, the day after.'

I was very excited that night, and did not sleep much. I heard some small sounds in the house; perhaps someone was awake. My room was large and comfortable. There was a little bed in it for Flora, but on my first night she slept with Mrs Grose. I woke up with the birds, and looked forward to my first full day with her.

When I arrived, the house was a pleasant surprise.

Flora showed me everything in the house and garden. She showed me the secret places, the old stairs, the empty rooms. After half an hour we were good friends.

'Perhaps,' I thought, 'I'm in some wonderful story. But, no, it's real, and it will be an adventure for me.'

I remembered my promise to my employer that evening. A letter came from Miles's school. I was not excited now, but worried. The head at the school wrote that Miles could not go back there again.

'They won't take him back!' I told Mrs Grose.

'Never?' she asked, surprised.

'Never. Here, you can read the letter.'

I gave it to her but she shook her head sadly.

'I cannot read,' she said. 'What has he done?' she was almost crying.

'They don't say. But they think that he's dangerous to the other children.'

'Dangerous?' Mrs Grose was angry now.

'Is he a bad child?'

'He's only ten years old! How can he be bad? Is she bad?' She pointed at Flora, who was sitting quietly at the table. The little girl was writing, practising her letter 'O's.

'Naughty, then?' I asked her.

'Oh yes, of course, he is sometimes naughty! But –'

'Every boy must be naughty sometimes.'

'Yes! A boy who is not naughty is not a boy for me!'

Later, before Miles arrived, I asked her about the last governess.

'What kind of lady was she?'

'She was young and pretty like you.'

'Was she careful with the boy?'

'With some things – yes. But perhaps not with everything. But she's dead now, so I mustn't speak badly of her.'

'Yes, of course,' I said, quickly. 'Was she ill? Did she die here?'

6

*The head at the school wrote that Miles could not go back there again.
'They won't take him back!' I told Mrs Grose.*

'He can't be bad! It's not possible! Look at him!'

'No, she went away for a holiday. Then she died – the master told me.'

'How did she die?'

'He didn't say.' And she would not tell me any more.

Miles was as beautiful as his sister. I loved him too, as soon as I saw him. He had a sweet innocence, and I could not understand the school's letter.

'He can't be bad! It's not possible!' I said to Mrs Grose later. 'Look at him!'

'Yes, I look at him all the time,' she smiled. 'What will you do?'

'I won't answer the letter. I can't write to his uncle. And I won't speak to Miles about it.'

'Good!' Mrs Grose said. 'Then together we'll be friends to the two children.' She kissed me like a sister.

Chapter 3 A Frightening Face

I did not give the children many lessons during those first weeks. Perhaps *they* were teaching *me* now – they were teaching me to laugh, to play, to be free. I was more innocent than the children. I know that now.

In the evenings, when they were in bed, I liked to walk among the summer flowers in the gardens, and under the old trees in the park. Sometimes I could see the face of my employer in front of my eyes. 'He's smiling at me,' I thought. 'He's pleased with me – I'm looking after the children well for him.'

One evening in June, I walked about three miles through the park. When I came back to the house, I looked up and saw a face. Was it my employer's face which I thought about so much? No, it was not – I realised that very quickly. A man stood on the roof of the tower. There were two towers, one at each end of the roof. Each tower had a room inside, and you could climb out onto the roof from them; Flora took me there on my first day. I did not know this man. I saw him very clearly, and he was watching me. He stood still and stared at me for a minute, then turned away.

I was frightened. Was there a secret in this old house? I wanted to ask Mrs Grose, but when I came back into the house, everything seemed quite ordinary again. I did not say anything to her, but for many days I thought about it. Finally I decided, 'It was a stranger who found a way into the house. But he's gone now, so I can forget him. I won't worry about it.'

I preferred to enjoy my days with the children. I was never bored with them. They were happy, and they made me happy too. I did not think about my family at home now; Flora and Miles were my family, and this was my home.

One Sunday, in the early evening, Mrs Grose and I decided to go to church together. My bag was in the dining-room, and I went in there to get it. Suddenly, I looked up and saw a face at the window. It was staring at me through the glass. It was the man who I saw on the roof. I stared at him; he stared at me. I did not know him, but I felt, strangely, that I knew him very well. Then he looked round the room.

'He's looking for someone, but not for me!' I realised.

Then I felt brave. I ran outside and looked for him. But he was not there. The garden was empty. I went back to the window, put my face against the glass, and stared in. Mrs Grose walked into the dining-room, and saw me. She turned white, and came outside to meet me.

'Why is *she* frightened?' I asked myself.

'What's the matter?' she asked me. 'Your face is white. You look terrible.'

'*My* face?' I said. 'I was frightened. You saw my face at the window, but when I was in the dining-room, I saw a man's face in the same place.'

'Who is he? Where has he gone?'

Suddenly, I looked up and saw a face at the window. It was staring at me through the glass.

'I have no idea.'

'Have you seen him before?'

'Yes – once. He was standing on the roof of the tower.'

'And you didn't tell me? What was he doing there?'

'He looked at me – that's all. He was a stranger, a dreadful man.'

Mrs Grose looked out over the gardens once more, then said, 'Well, it's time for church now.'

'No, I can't go to church. Not now. I can't leave the children. It's not safe.'

'It isn't safe?' she asked.

'He's dangerous!' I replied.

She realised something then. I could see it in her face.

'What did he look like?' she asked.

'He is like nobody!'

'What do you mean?'

'He has no hat!' She looked worried, so I continued quickly, 'He has red hair, and a long face, with strange eyes.'

Mrs Grose's mouth was open, and she stared at me. Is he handsome? How is he dressed?'

'Oh, yes, he's handsome. And he's wearing another person's clothes.'

'The master's!' she said.

'You know this man?'

She did not reply for a second, then she answered, 'Quint. Peter Quint. He was the master's servant. He took some of his clothes – but never his hat. When the master left, Quint looked after everything in the house. He was only a servant, but he gave the orders.'

'Then where did he go?'

'Go?' she said. 'Oh no, he died.'

'Died?' I almost screamed.

'Yes,' she said. 'Peter Quint is dead.'

Chapter 4   Two People Who Died

Mrs Grose and I talked a lot about Quint's ghost.

'I have never seen anything,' she said. But she knew my story was true. 'Who was he looking for?' she asked me.

'He was looking for little Miles,' I said, because suddenly I knew that it was true.

Mrs Grose looked frightened. 'The child?' she asked.

'His ghost wants to find the children.'

'How do you know?'

'I know, I know! And you know too, don't you?' She did not answer, so I continued, 'Miles never speaks about Quint. Isn't that strange? He says nothing to me. "They were great friends, Miles and Quint," you told me.'

'It was Quint's idea,' Mrs Grose said. 'He wanted to play with Miles all the time. He was too free with him.'

'Too free!' He was too free with my boy! – this was terrible.

'He was too free with everyone.'

'So he was truly a bad man?'

'I knew it, but the master didn't. He didn't like to hear about any sort of trouble. I couldn't tell him. I was afraid.'

'What were you afraid of?'

'Quint was so clever – he could do terrible things.'

'A dreadful man, with those innocent little children – couldn't you do something?'

'I couldn't say anything. Peter Quint gave the orders.' She began to cry.

Did Mrs Grose tell me everything? No – there was something that she didn't say. I had to be brave. I had to watch carefully. The children must not meet this ghost!

And then, one afternoon, I took Flora out into the garden. Miles was reading inside, so Flora and I walked down to the lake together. It was hot, and we walked under the trees for much of the time. When we arrived at the lake, I sat down with a book, and for an hour everything was quiet. Suddenly I thought, 'Someone is watching us.' But I did not look up at once. I looked at Flora first. She had stopped playing and was very still. 'She can see the person too!' I thought. Then she turned away quickly from the lake.

Now I had to look up. A woman was standing on the other side of the lake – a dreadful woman, dressed in black. She was staring at Flora. I knew that she was the ghost of Miss Jessel, the children's old governess.

'Flora saw her too!' I told Mrs Grose later.

'Did she tell you?' Mrs Grose asked.

'No – and that makes it more terrible! The woman has come for Flora. The way she looks at her –'

Mrs Grose turned white. 'She was dressed in black?'

'Yes, and she was handsome. She was a beautiful woman, but a bad one.'

'They were both bad,' she said at last.

'You must tell me about them now,' I said.

'They were – together,' she said. 'They were lovers. But she paid a terrible price for it. Yes, she suffered, poor woman! He did what he wanted.'

'With her?'

'With them all.'

'How did she die?'

'I don't know. I didn't want to know. But she couldn't stay in the house after that. She had to leave. She was a lady, and he was only a servant.'

'And Peter Quint? How did he die?'

'He drank too much one night. He came out of the bar in the village and fell down on the ice. He cut his head on a stone. Well, that's what people say. Nobody really knows.'

'It's all so terrible!' And now I began to cry, and Mrs Grose took me in her arms. 'We can't save the children! They're lost! Lost!'

14

A woman was standing on the other side of the lake — a dreadful woman, dressed in black.

But I still wanted to be with the children most of all, specially with Flora. She looked into my face carefully with her big, blue eyes, and said, 'You were crying.' She was so sweet, so innocent – how could she know about these dreadful things?

And Miles? I asked Mrs Grose about Miles. ' "He was sometimes bad," you said to me. How was he bad?'

'Naughty,' she replied. 'I said naughty, not bad.'

'Please tell me!' I continued. 'He's always so good with me. So when he was bad – or naughty – it was unusual. What happened?'

We were talking late into the night, and now the grey light of morning was coming. Mrs Grose was silent for a minute, then she answered me.

'Quint and the boy were together all the time. I didn't like it. I spoke to Miss Jessel about it. She was angry with me. "It's none of your business," she said. So I spoke to Miles.'

'You told him that Peter Quint was only a servant?'

'Yes. "You're only a servant too," he answered me. And there were times when he and Peter Quint were together for hours, but he said, "I haven't seen Peter today." '

'He lied to you?'

Mrs Grose seemed surprised by this word. 'Yes – perhaps he did.'

'And he knew about Quint, and Miss Jessel?'

'I don't know – I don't know!'

'Yes, you *do* know! And we need to know more!'

Chapter 5   The Children in Danger

I waited and watched carefully for some days. The children were so lovable and happy that I nearly forgot my worries sometimes. They enjoyed studying, and were clever and funny in our lessons together. Sometimes they seemed to have a plan: one of them talked to me, while the other disappeared outside. But this did not really worry me.

Then, one evening, I stayed up very late in my bedroom. I was reading a book by the light of a candle. Flora was asleep in her little bed in the corner. Suddenly, I looked up and listened. Something was moving in the house. I remembered my first night, when I heard sounds like this.

I took my candle and left the room. I locked the door behind me, and walked to the top of the stairs. My candle went out, but I noticed that it was already quite light, and I could see without it. I realised that there was someone on the stairs below. It was Peter Quint again. There was a big window by the stairs, he stood by it and stared up at me. I knew then that he was both wicked and dangerous. But I was not afraid. We stood and stared silently, and that was the strangest thing. A murderer can talk, but a ghost cannot. Then he turned, and disappeared at the bottom of the stairs.

I returned to my room. A candle was still burning there, and I saw that Flora's bed was empty. I ran to her bed, frightened. Then I heard a sound. She was hiding by the window. She looked very serious.

'You naughty person! Where did you go?'

I sat down, and she climbed onto my knee.

'Were you looking for me out of the window?' I asked her. 'Did you think I was in the garden?'

'Well, someone was out there,' she said, and smiled at me. Her face was innocent and beautiful in the candlelight.

'And did you see anybody?'

'Oh, no!'

I knew that she was lying. But I did not say anything.

Each night now I sat up late. Sometimes I went out of my room to look, and listen. Once I saw a woman on the stairs. She sat there in sadness, with her head in her hands. She did not show me her face, but I knew that it was dreadful and that she was

Flora was standing by the window . . . There was a full moon, and I could see her face in its light.

suffering. I only saw her for a second, and then she disappeared.

After eleven nights, I could not stay awake late, and I went to sleep quite early. I woke up at about one o'clock in the morning. Flora was standing by the window, staring out. She did not notice me. There was a full moon, and I could see her face in its light. She was giving herself to something out there, to the ghost that we saw by the lake. I got up – I wanted to find another room with windows that looked out onto the garden.

The room in the tower was the best one. It was a big, cold bedroom, nobody ever slept there. I put my face against the glass of the window. The garden was very bright in the moonlight. Somebody was standing on the grass and staring up above me – at the tower. So there was another person out there, on the roof of the tower. But the person in the garden was not the ghost of the woman. It was little Miles.

When I went down into the garden, Miles came in quietly with me, back to his bedroom.

'Tell me now, Miles,' I said. 'Why did you go out? What were you doing in the garden?'

'Will you understand?' he asked me, with his wonderful smile. I felt almost sick while I waited to hear. He planned to tell me everything!

'Well,' he said. 'I wanted to be bad!' He kissed me. 'I didn't go to bed! I went out at midnight! When I'm bad, I'm really bad!' He spoke like a naughty, happy child. 'I planned it with Flora.'

'She stood at the window –'

'To wake you up!'

'And you stood outside in the cold. Well, you must go to bed now.' I was the governess again, and Miles was just a naughty boy. He was too clever for me.

I told Mrs Grose everything. 'We think that the children are good, but they're not. They live with *them* – not with us. They want to be with Quint and that woman!'

'They're still here! Their ghosts are looking for our children.'

'But why?' Mrs Grose asked.

'Because Peter Quint and Miss Jessel are wicked, and they taught Flora and Miles to love wickedness. They're bad!'

'Yes, they were a wicked pair,' Mrs Grose said. 'But what can they do now? They're dead.'

'They're still here! Their ghosts are looking for our children. They can still take Miles and Flora from us!'

'Oh, my goodness!'

'They wait in high, strange or dangerous places – the roof of the tower, the other side of the lake. It's dangerous but exciting, for Flora and Miles. They'll try to get to those wicked people.'

'And a terrible accident can happen – I see,' said Mrs Grose. 'We must stop this. Their uncle must take them away from here. I can't write, so you must write to him.'

'What can I say? How will he know that it's true?' ('My employer will be angry with me,' I thought. 'I wanted so much to be brave and to help him.')

Mrs Grose took my arm. 'He must come!' she said. 'He must come back and help us!'

Chapter 6   A Letter to Miles's Uncle

The summer changed into the autumn. I didn't see any more ghosts, and I did nothing. The sky was grey, and dead leaves blew onto the grass. Did the children see things? Sometimes everything suddenly went quiet in the schoolroom. I think that wicked pair were with us then. I think, too, that the children could see them. But usually, they were happy and worked hard. They were very interested in their uncle.

'Will he come soon?' they asked me. They wrote beautiful letters to him.

'We can't send them to him,' I explained. 'He's too busy. Perhaps he'll come later in the year.'

I wanted to speak to the children about the ghosts, but I couldn't find a way. They stayed silent about them, and so did I. Sometimes, alone, I thought about it all night, but my thoughts stayed secret. Everything felt heavy, like a storm was coming.

Then the storm came. I was walking to church one Sunday morning with Miles. Flora and Mrs Grose were in front. It was bright, cold autumn weather now.

'Can you tell me,' Miles said, 'when I'm going back to school?'

His voice was sweet, but the words surprised me. I stopped suddenly. He smiled at me. 'I'm a boy, you know. And I'm getting older now. I'm with a lady all the time – is it a good idea? She's a wonderful lady, of course – but a boy needs other boys and men.'

We walked on now. 'Were you happy at school?' I asked him.

He thought for a second. 'Oh, I'm happy enough anywhere.'

'Then you must be happy here too!'

'Yes, but I want – I want more interesting things to see and do.'

'I see,' I said.

'Does my uncle know about me, about everything?'

'I don't think he's interested, Miles,' I answered.

'Then he must come and visit us!'

'Who will ask him?'

'I will!' Miles said.

We were at the church now, but I did not go in. I stayed outside. For the first time, I did not want to be with Miles. Of course, he was right – it was unnatural for a boy to spend all his time with a governess, every day. And I was doing nothing about it. Could I speak to his uncle? Miles knew now that I did not want to do this.

'He'll use it in his plan!' I thought. He and Flora looked

'Can you tell me,' Miles said, 'when I'm going back to school?'

innocent, but they were not. 'I must leave this house! I'll go back and get ready. I can leave today!'

In the house, I went up to the school room for my books. I opened the door. But there, sitting at my table, was that dreadful woman – Miss Jessel. She was writing – I knew it – to her lover, Quint. Her tired face was full of suffering. She was using my pen, my paper. She stood up, and for a few seconds she looked at me. I stared at her, then I screamed, 'You're a wicked, terrible woman!' She seemed to hear me. But the next minute the room was empty. And I knew now that I must stay in the house. I could not leave.

'I've talked to Miss Jessel,' I said to Mrs Grose later, by the fire.

Mrs Grose was surprised, but she stayed calm. 'And what did she say?'

'She's suffering. She wants Flora. I've decided to write to the children's uncle.'

'Oh yes!' Mrs Grose said. 'You must.'

'I'll tell him this,' I said. ' "I cannot teach a boy who is wicked. The school have sent him home because of his wickedness." '

'But – we don't know –'

'Yes, we do,' I said. 'He *seems* to be so good, that he *must* be wicked, really wicked. I'll write tonight!'

I began the letter that evening. There was a strong wind and heavy rain outside. But it was quiet in my room, and Flora was asleep in her little bed. I stood up, took my candle and went to Miles's bedroom door. I listened. He called out, 'Come in! I can hear you outside!'

He was awake but in bed.

'Aren't you sleeping?' I asked him.

'No,' he answered, quite happily. 'I like to lie and think.'

'What do you think about?'

'About you, of course! And about all these strange things –'

'What strange things?'

24

*She stood up, and for a few seconds she looked at me. I stared at her,
then I screamed.*

'Oh, you know!'

I held his hand, and he smiled up at me. 'Of course you can go back to school,' I said. 'But we must find a new one for you.' He looked so young, and innocent in his bed. 'You didn't say anything before,' I continued. 'What do you really want?'

He shook his head. 'I want to go away! Oh – you know what a boy wants!'

Do I? 'You want to go to your uncle?' I asked him.

'He must come here.'

'Yes, but he'll take you away, Miles.'

'That's what I want! You must tell him everything.'

'Tell him what?' I asked. 'He'll ask you questions. You must tell him things, too.'

'What things?'

'The things that you don't tell me. He must decide on his plans for you. You can't go back to your old school, you know.'

I looked at this brave, calm, young boy, and I kissed him with love.

'I'm writing to your uncle,' I said. 'I've already started the letter.'

'Well then, finish it!'

'Tell me something first, Miles. What happened?' He looked at me, surprised. 'What happened here in this house? What happened at school?' He was still looking at me. I held my arms out to him.

'Oh Miles!' I said. 'Dear little Miles, I want to help you! I don't want to hurt you. I want to help you so much!' But I knew at once that this was a mistake. Suddenly, there was a loud and terrible noise, a crash against the window. The cold wind blew into the room. Miles screamed.

I jumped up. Everything was dark.

'The candle has gone out!' I said.

'I blew it out, my dear,' Miles said.

I looked at this brave, calm, young boy, and I kissed him with love.

Chapter 7   Flora Disappears

After the children's lessons the next day, Mrs Grose asked me, 'Have you written the letter?'

'Yes, I've written it.' I did not tell her that it was still in my pocket. I had to send it, I knew that now. Later, I put it on the table by the front door. 'One of the servants will find it, and take it to town,' I thought.

In the afternoon, Miles came to me. 'Shall I play some music for you?' he asked. He knew that he was winning, and that he was free now. He did not need to fight me, he could be friendly. The music was strange and beautiful. I was almost asleep. When it finished, I jumped up.

'Where's Flora?' I asked.

'How do I know?' Miles replied. He laughed, and started to play again.

I looked in my room, but Flora was not there. I went to Mrs Grose. Mrs Grose did not know where she was.

'Perhaps she's in one of the empty rooms,' she said. 'I thought that she was with you.'

Usually, I stayed with Flora all the time. 'No, she's outside, somewhere quite far away,' I answered. Mrs Grose looked surprised.

'Without a hat?' she asked.

'That woman that doesn't wear a hat!' I said. 'She's with *her*! We must find them!'

Mrs Grose did not move. 'And where is Miles?'

'Oh, *he's* with Quint in the schoolroom! He stayed with me so that Flora could get away! He's free now, he can do what he likes.'

We stood by the front door. The afternoon was grey, and the grass was wet.

'You aren't wearing your outdoor clothes!' Mrs Grose said.

'It doesn't matter! Flora hasn't got outdoor clothes on either,' I replied. 'I can't wait to dress! If you want to dress you must stay behind! Look for Flora upstairs!'

'And see *him*?' was her frightened reply. She came outside with me at once.

We walked quickly to the lake. I was sure that Flora was there.

'She wanted to go back there alone,' I explained to Mrs Grose. 'She and Miles planned this. And I'm sure that Miss Jessel is by the lake now.'

We arrived at the lake, but we could not see Flora.

'She's taken the boat,' I said, 'and hidden it on the other side. We must walk round and find her!'

'How could she do all that? She's only a little girl!'

'No, sometimes she's an old, old woman,' I said. 'And there's someone with her. You'll see.'

Ten minutes later, we arrived at the other side of the lake, and found the boat there. But where was Flora? We went on, into the next field.

'There she is!' we both said at the same time.

Flora stood on the grass and smiled. She did not move or speak. She smiled and smiled, in a dreadful, silent way. Mrs Grose threw her arms round the child.

Flora stared in surprise at my head, without its hat, and said, 'Where are your outdoor things?'

'Where are yours?' I asked her.

'And where's Miles?' she asked.

'If you'll tell me, I'll tell you –' There must be no secrets now.

'Tell you what?'

'Tell me, my dear – Where's Miss Jessel?'

Mrs Grose gave a small scream. In the same second, I screamed too – I shook Mrs Grose's arm and said, 'She's there, she's there!'

Miss Jessel stood on the other side of the lake. In a way, I was glad. 'It's all true, then,' I thought. 'Mrs Grose will be able to see everything, too.'

I shook Mrs Grose's arm and said, 'She's there, she's there!'

I pointed across the lake. Mrs Grose looked, but Flora did not. She watched my face calmly and seriously.

'She's there, you poor unhappy child! You can see her very well!'

But Mrs Grose was angry, 'What terrible things you say! Where can you see someone? There's nobody there!'

She could not see anything! And now I was losing everything! That wicked governess was winning!

'She's not there,' Mrs Grose continued, talking to Flora now. 'You can't see anyone! That poor lady – poor Miss Jessel's dead – we know that, don't we? It's all a mistake, and we're going home now, quickly.'

Flora was holding on to Mrs Grose's dress. Her face was suddenly ugly. 'I can't see anybody! I never see anything! I don't like you.' She turned towards Mrs Grose. 'Take me away from her!'

'From *me*?' I asked.

'From you – from you!'

I stared at the ghost, which was still there. Then I shook my head and said sadly to Flora, 'I've lost you. I'm sorry. She's won. I tried to help you. Goodbye.' And to Mrs Grose I said, 'Go! Go at once!'

I don't remember anything after that. I was on the ground, crying, for a very long time. It was nearly evening when I got up. I went back to the house and up to my room. Flora's things weren't there now. Later, Miles came and sat silently with me. He was not unfriendly. I was very cold, but felt warm when he was there.

Chapter 8   Trying to Save Miles

Mrs Grose came into my room the next morning. Flora was ill.

'What does she say?' I asked. 'What has she seen?'

'I can't ask her,' Mrs Grose said sadly. 'But she seems so old now.'

'Does she talk about Miss Jessel?'

'Not a word.'

'They're so clever, that woman and Flora! Flora will never speak to me again. And she'll tell her uncle about me. "What a terrible governess!" he'll think. Shall I leave now?' I continued. 'That's what Flora wants, isn't it?'

She agreed. 'She doesn't want to see you again.'

'Well then,' I said, '*you* must go. You must take Flora away, to her uncle's. I'll stay here with Miles. But the two children must not meet alone together! Not for three seconds!'

'Yes, you're right. Flora must leave this house. We'll go this morning. And – I can't stay! Flora is saying such terrible things. Dreadful words, dreadful things. Where did she learn them?'

She was crying now. 'You believe me, then?' I asked her.

'Oh, yes, I do! I must take Flora far away, far from *them*!' she said.

'My letter – it will arrive in town first,' I said.

She shook her head. 'No, it won't. It's disappeared.'

'What do you mean?'

'It disappeared from the table by the front door. The other servants haven't seen it. Miles –'

'Miles took it?' This was terrible. 'Then he's read it! So he's a thief – he was stealing letters at school, then! I must talk to him. If he talks to me, we can save him!'

The servants were surprised when Flora left with Mrs Grose. They stared at me silently when I walked through the house. But Miles did not seem worried. We ate lunch together in the large dining-room.

'Is Flora very ill?' he asked me.

'She'll get better in London. Take some meat, Miles,' I said.

He filled his plate, and we ate quickly. Miles got up, and stood with his back to me and his hands in his little pockets. We did not speak while the servant took the plates away.

'Flora is saying such terrible things. Dreadful words, dreadful things.'

'Well,' Miles said. 'We're alone now!'

'Not quite alone,' I answered.

'Of course, there are the others,' he said. 'But they're not important, are they?' He walked to the window and put his face against the glass. Was he looking for something, or somebody?

'Have you enjoyed yourself today?' I asked.

'Oh, yes! I'm so free now. I walked miles and miles. I went everywhere.'

'And do you like it?'

'Do you?' he replied. '*You* are more alone now.'

'It doesn't matter,' I said. 'I'm happy to be here. And why am I still here? For you, of course.'

He stared at me, and his little face was both handsome and serious.

'You're staying here just for me?'

'Yes. I'm your friend, and I want to help you – I told you so, that night, in your bedroom. Do you remember?'

'Yes, but you wanted something from me, too!'

'Yes. Tell me everything, Miles. That's what I want!'

'Ah! You're staying here so that I can tell you everything!'

'Well, yes, it's true.'

'Now?' he asked.

'It's a good time. Or do you want to go out again?'

'Yes, I want to go out very much!' He picked up his hat, and was ready to leave. 'I'll tell you everything – I promise. But later – not now.'

'Why not now?'

He turned to the window again and was silent. 'I have to see the gardener,' he said. He was lying, I knew it. Someone was waiting for him outside.

'Well, then,' I said. 'Tell me just one little thing before you go. Did you take my letter from the table by the door?'

'Well,' Miles said. 'We're alone now!'

Then, in that same second, I saw the terrible face of Peter Quint at the window again. The room changed, and everything felt bad. But Miles saw nothing.

'Yes, I took it,' he said.

I took him in my arms. He could not see the ghost, and he was not lying now! These were two good, good things! The face still stared at us through the glass.

'Why did you take it?'

'I wanted to know what you wrote about me,' he said.

'And did you open the letter?' I asked.

'I opened it, and then I burnt it,' he said.

'And did you do this at school? Did you steal letters, and burn them? Did you steal other things, Miles?'

'*Me?*' he asked. '*Steal?*' His voice told me that this was a terrible question.

My face was red. 'Well, why can't you go back? What did you do, then?'

'I – I said things,' the boy replied, 'to a few people. And then all the masters heard about it. That's all.'

'What things?' I asked. But he didn't say. Perhaps he really was innocent!

'Didn't they tell you? Well, there *were* some bad things. Perhaps they were too bad for a letter.'

But the face at the window came closer. It wanted to stop Miles, to stop his true answers. I screamed and held Miles again. 'No more, no more!' I shouted to the ghost.

'Is *she* here?' Miles asked, and turned his eyes to the window. But he could still see nothing.

'She?' I asked.

'Miss Jessel, Miss Jessel!' he shouted in anger.

I understood then; he was thinking about Flora's story.

'No, it's not Miss Jessel. But that other dreadful face – that wicked man – he's at the window *for the last time*!'

36

I saw the terrible face of Peter Quint at the window again . . .
But Miles saw nothing.

I realised what I was holding. I was holding a dead child, not a living one.

He got angrier then, and the room felt worse. '*He* is here then?' he asked.

'Who?' I had to ask him.

'Peter Quint, of course! Where is he?' He looked round the room. 'Where?'

'It doesn't matter!' I said. 'I have you now! You are mine, not his! He has lost you for ever! There, there!' I pointed. But Miles saw nothing. He screamed like an animal, like a person who has lost everything. 'He's falling!' I thought. 'I must catch him and save him!' I held him hard, very hard. And then Miles and I were alone, alone together in a quiet afternoon. But suddenly, his little heart stopped, and I realised what I was holding. I was holding a dead child, not a living one.

ACTIVITIES

Chapter 1

Before you read

1 Look at the Word List at the back of the book.

    a Find five words for people.

    b Find four words that can describe people or things.

    c Find two words for doing things.

    d Find one word for a strong feeling.

2 Complete the sentences with words from the Word List.

    a It was very dark so I lit a ..... .

    b From the top of the ..... , everything looked very small.

    c This is very important. Please call your mother ..... .

    d 'Of course it wasn't a ..... ! Dead people can't come back to life.'

    e '..... ! What a surprise!'

    f I turned the ..... three more times until it was tight.

    g I couldn't see my friend ..... the group of people.

    h We can't go back. We have to go ..... .

3 Read the Introduction and answer these questions.

    a Do you find out the name of the governess?

    b What is the housekeeper called?

    c Who are Miles and Flora?

    d Are Peter Quint and Miss Jessel alive?

    e Where did Henry James spend more of his life – in America or England?

    f How is *The Turn of the Screw* different from Henry James's other stories?

    g Do you think that children are always innocent?

    h Do you believe in ghosts?

4 Complete each sentence with the correct word.

again   brother   died   friends   ghost

governess   job   loved   problems

Douglas knows a very frightening (a)......................... story about two children. His sister's (b)......................... wrote the story down a long time ago. Before he starts to read it, Douglas tells his (c)......................... about the governess. Her first (d)......................... was for a rich man. She went to look after the children of this man's (e)......................... in the country. She was nervous about the job because the last governess (f)......................... . But she took the job because she (g)......................... her new master. He told her never to ask him about any (h)......................... with the children. She never saw her boss (i)......................... .

After you read

5 Work in pairs and have this conversation between the governess and the master.

Student A: You're the governess. Ask the master about the job, the children, the house, the last governess and the other people working at the house.

Student B: You're the master. Answer the governess's questions. Tell her never to ask you for help with the children.

Chapters 2–3

Before you read

6 Discuss these questions. What do you think?

a Will the governess like the house?

b What will Flora be like?

c Will Mrs Grose be friendly?

d Look at the pictures and words on pages 7 and 8. Will we find out why Miles's school doesn't want him?

e Look at the picture on page 11. Is it a man or a ghost?

7 Circle the correct words in *italics*.

    a Mrs Grose and Flora seem *friendly / unfriendly*.

    b Miles is in serious trouble *at school / with his uncle*.

    c The new *governess / school* won't take him back.

    d Mrs Grose *reads / doesn't read* the letter from the school.

    e Mrs Grose says Miles is sometimes *naughty / dangerous*.

    f The governess *is / isn't* going to tell Miles's uncle about the letter.

8 Are the sentences right (✓) or wrong (✗)?

    a The governess spends all her time teaching and working. .....

    b One day she sees a woman on the tower just for a minute. .....

    c Another day she sees a man looking through a window. .....

    d She isn't very frightened. .....

    e Mrs Grose says she knows the man. .....

After you read

9 Discuss these questions. What do you think?

    a Did Miles do anything wrong at school? What?

    b Should the governess write to the master about Miles?

    c Is the governess doing a good job, or should she spend more time teaching the children?

    d Do you think only some people can see ghosts?

    e Is or was Peter Quint bad for the children?

Chapter 4

Before you read

10 Do you think the governess is going to see any more ghosts?

11 Look at the picture on page 15. Who is the woman in black?

12 Complete the sentences. Write one word in each space.

    a The governess says Quint is .... for Miles.

    b Mrs Grose says Quint was too .... with Miles.

    c Near the .... the governess sees the ghost of Miss Jessel.

    d Miss Jessel was the last ....

    e She and Peter Quint were ....

    f The governess says Flora also saw Miss Jessel's ....

    g Mrs Grose says Miles was sometimes .... but not bad.

After you read

13 Answer the questions. What do you think?

    a Did Flora really see the ghost or not?

    b Do we know how Quint and Miss Jessel were 'bad'?

    c Do you think the governess is strange? Why or why not?

Chapter 5

Before you read

14 Do you think the governess will see the ghosts again? What about Mrs Grose: will she see them too?

While you read

15 Are the sentences right (✓) or wrong (✗)?

    a One night the governess sees Quint's ghost on the stairs.   .....

    b Miles is standing and talking with the ghost.   .....

    c The governess is sure that Flora sometimes tells lies.   .....

    d The governess always sleeps well at night.   .....

    e One night she sees Flora in the garden at midnight.   .....

    f She's sure Miles is looking up at a ghost on the tower.   .....

    g Miles says they were playing a game to make her worried.   .....

    h The governess thinks the children will do something dangerous because of the ghosts.   .....

    i Mrs Grose doesn't want the uncle to come and help.   .....

After you read

16 Work in pairs. Have this conversation between Flora and Miles about their governess. They know she watches them a lot. They want her to get worried. They are planning a game.

> *Student A:* You are Miles. Talk about the governess. Tell Flora to get up at night and look out of the window. Tell her why.
>
> *Student B:* You are Flora. Ask Miles when to get up. Ask him how the game will work.

Chapter 6

Before you read

17 Look at the picture and read the words on page 23.

    a Why do you think Miles wants to go back to school?

    b Is it better for children to study at home or at school?

While you read

18 Circle the correct words in *italics*.

    a The children *want / don't* want their uncle to visit.

    b Miles *wants / doesn't* want to go back to school.

    c The governess wants to *keep / leave* her job.

    d She sees Miss Jessel in the *school room / tower*.

    e She thinks Miss Jessel wants *Miles / Flora*.

    f She is sure Miles is *seriously bad / a bit naughty*.

    g She goes into Miles's room one *afternoon / night*.

    h She wants to know about his old *school / friends*.

    i Miles *wants / doesn't* want her to write to his uncle.

After you read

19 Discuss these questions. What do you think?

    a Why does Miles want to go back to school?

    b Why doesn't the governess want him to go?

    c Is Miles a seriously bad child? Why or why not?

Chapter 7

Before you read

20 Do you think the governess will write to the uncle?

21 Look at the picture on page 30. The governess is looking at Miss Jessel's ghost. Will Flora and Mrs Grose also see it?

While you read

22 Who says these things?

a	'Have you written the letter?'	....
b	'Where's Flora?'	....
c	'How do I know?'	....
d	'And where is Miles?'	....
e	'Oh, he's with Quint in the schoolroom!'	....
f	'She's taken the boat and hidden it.'	....
g	'She's only a little girl.'	....

23 Complete the sentences with the correct words.

asks   cries   ghost   ground   secrets   take   well   women

The two (a)......................... find Flora on the other side of the lake. The governess says Flora must tell her all her (b)......................... She (c)......................... her where Miss Jessel is. Suddenly the governess sees the (d)......................... , but the other two don't see it. The governess says that Flora can see Miss Jessel very (e)......................... . But Flora asks Mrs Grose to (f)......................... her away from the governess. The governess falls on the (g)......................... and (h)......................... for a long time.

After you read

24 Discuss these questions.

a Do you think Flora and Mrs Grose could see Miss Jessel?

b Why did Mrs Grose get angry with the governess?

c What does the governess mean when she says, 'I've lost you. I'm sorry. She's won. I tried to help you.'

Chapter 8

Before you read

25 Look at the picture and the words on page 35. Where do you think Flora and Mrs Grose have gone?

26 Discuss these questions. What do you think?

   a Is it safe for the children to stay at the house? Why (not)?

   b Should the governess leave her job? Why or why not?

While you read

27 Choose the correct ending for each sentence.

   a Flora refuses to *go to her uncle's / see the governess again*.

   b Mrs Grose and Flora leave to *see the uncle / find a school*.

   c The governess wants Miles to *write letters / tell her everything*.

   d The governess sees Quint *with Miss Jessel / but Miles doesn't*.

   e She finds out that Miles has *burnt / posted* her letter.

   f She suggests that at school Miles *hit children / stole things*.

   g Miles says he only *said some bad things / told a lot of lies*.

   h Miles tries to see Peter Quint, *but can't / and does at last*.

   i At the end of the story Miles is *asleep / dead*.

After you read

28 Discuss these questions. What do you think?

   a Why does Miles die? Does the ghost or the governess kill Miles, or is it an accident?

   b Is the governess a crazy woman with a sick mind? Or are there bad ghosts who want to steal the children?

29 Work in pairs. Have this conversation.

   Student A: You are Flora's uncle. Ask why Mrs Grose and Flora have come to London. Ask about Miles.

   Student B: You are Mrs Grose. Answer the uncle's questions. Tell him about the governess and the ghosts, and about Miles.

Writing

30 Write the uncle's notice in a newspaper, asking for a governess for Miles and Flora. Give information about the job, the house, the children, the money, the rules.

31 Write a letter from the governess to the uncle. She has seen the notice and is interested in the job. She tells the uncle about herself and asks for more information.

32 Write about this book. Tell some but not all of the story. Describe the best things about the book. Start like this: *This is a story about two children and their governess . . .*

33 You are the governess in Chapter 2. Write a letter to a friend. Write about the job – the handsome boss, the nice house, the friendly housekeeper, the money, the beautiful children. Write about your one worry – Miles and his school.

34 You are the governess. Write in your private notebook about the first time that you saw the strange man on the tower. Describe your day with the children and your evening walk in the park. Say why you didn't tell anyone about the man.

35 Write a conversation between Mrs Grose and the cook about the governess. The cook thinks the governess is strange. Mrs Grose is kind about her.

36 Imagine a servant calls the police after Miles's death. Write a newspaper report. Start like this: *The police were called to the home of . . .*

37 In Chapter 5, Miles and Flora plan to be naughty in the night. Write a conversation between Miles and Flora. They talk about the governess and make plans.

38 Imagine that after Miles's death the governess visits a doctor. She tells him about the ghosts and the children. The doctor doesn't believe in ghosts. Write their conversation.

39 Write the letter that the governess writes to her employer in Chapter 6.

WORD LIST

among (prep) in a group of

anger (n) the feeling of being angry

at once (adv) immediately

blow (v) When the wind *blows*, the air moves. The past form is **blew**

candle (n) a stick that you burn to produce light

dreadful (adj) very bad or unpleasant

forward (adv) towards a place that is in front

ghost (n) a dead person who, some people believe, comes back to the world without his/her body.

goodness! (n) a word that some people use to show surprise

governess (n) a woman who lives with a family and teaches their children at home

housekeeper (n) somebody who cleans and cooks in a house or hotel

innocent (adj) not knowing much about life or about bad things.

master (n) an old word meaning a man who employed other people

naughty (adj) like a bad child

screw (n) a piece of metal that you turn to tighten something

servant (n) somebody who works for a person or family in their home

stare (v) to look at somebody or something for a long time

stranger (n) somebody who you do not know

tower (n) a tall narrow building or part of a building

wicked (adj) very bad or doing very bad things